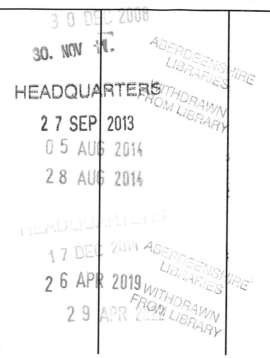
WODEHOUSE, P. G.

The wit & wisdom of
P.G. Wodehouse

The
Wit and Wisdom
of
P. G. Wodehouse

Compiled and edited by
Tony Ring

arrow books

Published by Arrow Books 2008

1 3 5 7 9 10 8 6 4 2

Copyright © The Trustees of the Estate of P.G. Wodehouse 2007
Selections and Introduction © Tony Ring 2007

First published in the United Kingdom in 2007 by Hutchinson

Arrow Books
The Random House Group Limited
20 Vauxhall Bridge Road, London, SW1V 2SA

www.rbooks.co.uk

Addresses for companies within The Random House Group Limited can
be found at: www.randomhouse.co.uk/offices.htm

The Random House Group Limited Reg. No. 954009

A CIP catalogue record for this book
is available from the British Library

ISBN 9780099522249

The Random House Group Limited supports The Forest Stewardship
Council (FSC), the leading international forest certification organisation.
All our titles that are printed on Greenpeace approved FSC certified paper
carry the FSC logo. Our paper procurement policy can be found at
www.rbooks.co.uk/environment

Print TD

INTRODUCTION

IN THE LATE 1930S, HILAIRE BELLOC described P. G. Wodehouse as 'the head of my profession', and demonstrated how he was able to present the laughable with mastery and skill using a method that the reader could not directly perceive. Evelyn Waugh, who likewise held him in awe as a master of the English language, concisely illustrated the point with his comment that Wodehouse produced three wholly original similes on each page.

Wodehouse was also a highly skilled plot-maker – his novels and short stories are complex and needed the most careful monitoring to ensure loose ends were tied up. Much of his humour evolved naturally from the plots and related dialogue, at which he was a master, so that the full richness can only be seen in context. As a result, we can include relatively few of the misquotations from the works of other authors at which he was so proficient.

Though not renowned for deep philosophical insights, his writing does contain many hidden truths, and our selection has been divided into quotations which are essentially funny and those which are more epigrammatic in nature. 'Wit' will be found on the verso, or left-hand pages; 'Wisdom' on the recto.

Wodehouse's humour was broadly based, and he took careful note of news reports and daily happenings with comic potential. These did not always reflect his personal views – as early as 1917, in *Piccadilly Jim*, he was referring to cigarettes as 'coffin-nails', though he was an inveterate pipe-smoker thoughout his life.

Some of his writing gains added humour with hindsight. In the first part of the the school story, *Mike* (1907 in magazine form), the opposing captains in the Wrykyn *v* Ripton cricket match were Burgess and Maclaine. That coincidence caused no ripple of excitement at the time, since Maclaine was spelt differently and the future Cambridge spies would not be born until 1911 and 1913 respectively, but it generates a smile today. As does the use of the name Anthony Blunt as the author of a book declaimed from the pulpit in the *Ladies Home Journal* publication of *Cocktail Time* in 1958, which for no apparent reason was changed to Richard Blunt for book publication!

One of the joys of Wodehouse is to find new humour in his works every time they are read. Whether you are a Wodehouse virgin, or come to this book for a refresher course, I hope you enjoy the experience, and that you are inspired to delve into his work more deeply.

The Wit and Wisdom of
P. G. WODEHOUSE

In order to make a song a smash, it is not enough for the singer to be on top of his form. The accompanist, also, must do his bit. And the primary thing a singer expects from his accompanist is that he shall play the accompaniment to the song he is singing.

(From 'The Masked Troubadour' in *Lord Emsworth and Others*)

It almost seemed as if another of my quick trips to America would be rendered necessary. About the only advantage of having an aunt like Aunt Agatha is that it makes one travel, thus broadening the mind and enabling one to see new faces.

(From *Joy in the Morning*, chapter 11)

[1]

There had been a period when, he being fifteen and she ten, Pat had lavished on him all the worship of a small girl for a big boy who can wiggle his ears and is not afraid of cows. But since then her attitude had changed. Her manner towards him nowadays alternated between that of a nurse towards a child who is not quite right in the head and that of the owner of a clumsy but rather likeable dog.

(From *Money for Nothing*, chapter 1)

Warm though the morning was, he shivered, as only a confirmed bachelor gazing into the naked face of matrimony can shiver.

(From *The Old Reliable*, chapter 1)

The Captain was on the bridge, pretty sure that he knew the way to New York but, just to be on the safe side, murmuring to himself 'Turn right at Cherbourg and then straight on.'

(From 'Life with Freddie' in *Plum Pie*)

Writers through the ages have made a good many derogatory remarks about money, and one gets the impression that it is a thing best steered clear of, but every now and then one finds people who like the stuff and one of these was Jane. It seemed to her to fill a long-felt want.

(From *The Girl in Blue*, chapter 11)

The adjective 'cross' as a description of the Jovelike wrath that consumed his whole being . . . jarred upon Derek profoundly. It was as though Prometheus, with the vultures tearing his liver, had been asked if he were piqued.

(From *Jill the Reckless*, chapter 4)

Rugby football is a game I can't claim absolutely to understand in all its niceties, if you know what I mean. I can follow the broad, general principles, of course. I mean to say, I know that the main scheme is to work the ball down the field somehow and deposit it over the line at the other end, and that, in order to squelch this programme, each side is allowed to put in a certain amount of assault and battery and do things to its fellow-man which, if done elsewhere, would result in fourteen days without the option, coupled with some strong remarks from the bench.

(From 'The Ordeal of Young Tuppy' in *Very Good, Jeeves*)

It is never difficult to distinguish between a Scotsman with a grievance and a ray of sunshine.

(From 'The Custody of a Pumpkin' in *Blandings Castle and Elsewhere*)

'My motto is "Love and let love" - with the one stipulation that people who love in glass-houses should breathe on the windows.'

(From the play *Come On, Jeeves*)

The best-laid plans of mice and men [finish] up on the cutting-room floor.

(From *Pearls, Girls and Monty Bodkin*, chapter 12)

The task of composing a sermon which should practically make sense and yet not be above the heads of his rustic flock was always one that caused Augustine Mulliner to concentrate tensely. Soon he was lost in his labour and oblivious to everything but the problem of how to find a word of one syllable that meant Supralapsarianism.

(From 'Gala Night' in *Mulliner Nights*)

'I won't believe you're married till I see the bishop and assistant clergy mopping their foreheads and saying, "Well, that's that. We've really got the young blighter off at last."'

(From *Aunts Aren't Gentlemen*, chapter 13)

'Have you any conception of what would happen were my wife to learn that I was a millionaire? Do you think I should be allowed to go on living in Valley Fields, the place I love, and continue to be a house-agent, the work I love? Do you suppose I should be permitted to keep my old friends, like Mr Wrenn of San Rafael, with whom I play chess on Saturdays, and feed rabbits in my shirt sleeves? No, I should be whisked off to a flat in Mayfair, I should have to spend long months in the south of France, a butler would be engaged and I should have to dress for dinner every night. I should have to join a London club, take a box at the opera, learn to play polo,' said Mr Cornelius, allowing his morbid fancy to run away with him a little.

(From *Ice in the Bedroom*, chapter 26)

[7]

[Beach the butler] was a man who had made two chins grow where only one had been before, and his waistcoat swelled like the sail of a racing yacht.

(From *Galahad at Blandings*, chapter 2)

The fourth hole found him four down, and one had the feeling that he was lucky not to be five.

(From 'Excelsior' in *Nothing Serious*)

He was in the acute stage of that malady which, for want of a better name, scientists call the heeby-jeebies.

(From *Spring Fever*, chapter 3)

He was a chartered accountant, and all chartered accountants have hearts as big as hotels. You think they're engrossed in auditing the half-yearly balance sheets of Miggs, Montagu and Murgatroyd, general importers, and all the time they're writing notes to blondes saying 'Tomorrow, one-thirty, same place.'

(From *Ice in the Bedroom*, chapter 7)

'What a curse these social distinctions are. They ought to be abolished. I remember saying that to Karl Marx once, and he thought there might be a book in it.'

(From *Quick Service*, chapter 9)

One felt immediately on seeing [Lady Constance] that there stood the daughter of a hundred earls, just as when confronted with Lord Emsworth one had the impression that one had encountered the son of a hundred tramp cyclists.

(From *A Pelican at Blandings*, chapter 1)

Unlike the male codfish, which, suddenly finding itself the parent of three million five hundred thousand little codfish, cheerfully resolves to love them all, the British aristocracy is apt to look with a somewhat jaundiced eye on its younger sons.

(From 'The Custody of the Pumpkin'
in *Blandings Castle and Elsewhere*)

'That's the way to get on in the world - by grabbing your opportunities. Why, what's Big Ben but a wrist-watch that saw its chance and made good.'

(From *The Small Bachelor*, chapter 6)

Like all young artists nowadays, he had always held before him as the goal of his ambition the invention of some new comic animal for the motion pictures. What he burned to do, as Velasquez would have burned to do if he had lived today, was to think of another Mickey Mouse and then give up work and watch the money roll in.

(From 'Buried Treasure' in *Lord Emsworth and Others*)

'She is the woman who is leading California out of the swamp of alcohol.'

'Good God!' I could tell by Eggy's voice that he was interested. 'Is there a swamp of alcohol in these parts? What an amazing country America is. Talk about every modern convenience. Do you mean you can simply go there and *lap*?'

(From *Laughing Gas*, chapter 9)

I remained motionless, like a ventriloquist's dummy whose ventriloquist has gone off to the local and left it sitting.

(From *Stiff Upper Lip, Jeeves*, chapter 14)

While still vague as to what exactly were the qualities he demanded in a wife, he was very clear in his mind that she must not be the sort of girl who routs a man out at midnight to go and pinch portraits and gets him bitten in the leg by Pekinese.

(From *Quick Service*, chapter 16)

Love, he felt, and he was a man who had thought about these things, should not manifest itself in such a strongly marked inclination, when in the presence of the adored object, to stand on one leg and twiddle the fingers.

(From *Money in the Bank*, chapter 1)

Nature, stretching Horace Davenport out, had forgotten to stretch him sideways, and one could have pictured Euclid, had they met, nudging a friend and saying 'Don't look now, but this chap coming along illustrates exactly what I was telling you about a straight line having length without breadth.'

(From *Uncle Fred in the Springtime*, chapter 1)

[Gloria Salt's] dark beauty made her look like a serpent of Old Nile. A nervous host, encountering her on her way to dine, might have been excused for wondering whether to offer her a dry martini or an asp.

(From *Pigs Have Wings*, chapter 3)

Reluctant though one may be to admit it, the entire British aristocracy is seamed and honeycombed with immorality . . . If you took a pin and jabbed it down anywhere in the pages of *Debrett's Peerage* you would find it piercing the name of someone who was going about the place with a conscience as tender as a sunburned neck.

(From 'The Smile That Wins' in *Mulliner Nights*)

Golf . . . is the infallible test. The man who can go into a patch of rough alone, with the knowledge that only God is watching him, and play his ball where it lies, is the man who will serve you faithfully and well.

(From 'Ordeal by Golf' in *The Clicking of Cuthbert*)

'. . . I assure you, on the word of an English gentleman, that this lady is a complete stranger to me.'

'Stranger?'

'A complete and total stranger.'

'Oh?' said the bloke. 'Then what's she doing sitting in your lap?'

(From 'Fate' in *Young Men in Spats*)

'I don't know if I am standing on my head or my heels.'

'Sift the evidence. At which end of you is the ceiling?'

(From *Cocktail Time*, chapter 23)

If the youth of America has a fault, it is that it is always a bit inclined, when something shapely looms up on the skyline, to let its mind wander from the business in hand.

(From 'Unpleasantness at Kozy Kot'
in *A Few Quick Ones* (US Edition))

Where one goes wrong when looking for the ideal girl is in making one's selection before walking the full length of the counter.

(From *Much Obliged, Jeeves*, chapter 13)

'The advice I give to every young man starting out to seek a life partner is to find a girl whom he can tickle.'

(From *Uncle Dynamite*, chapter 2)

Years before, when a boy, and romantic as most boys are, his lordship had sometimes regretted that the Emsworths, though an ancient clan, did not possess a Family Curse. How little he had suspected that he was shortly to become the father of it.

(From 'Lord Emsworth Acts for the Best'
in *Blandings Castle and Elsewhere*)

Observing what it was that Bingo was carrying, Oofy backed hastily.

'Hey!' he exclaimed. 'Don't point that thing at me!'

'It's only my baby.'

'I dare say. But point it the other way.'

(From 'Leave It To Algy' in *A Few Quick Ones*)

One of the advantages of being sparing in one's acts of heroism is that it makes them easy to remember.

(From *Bill the Conqueror*, chapter 3)

He was one of those young men who must be heirs or nothing. This is the age of the specialist, and years ago Rollo had settled on his career. Even as a boy, hardly capable of connected thought, he had been convinced that his speciality, the one thing he could do really well, was to inherit money. All he wanted was a chance. It would be bitter if Fate should withhold it from him.

(From 'Ahead of Schedule' in *The Man Upstairs*)

Her smile seemed to make the world on the instant a sweeter and better place. Policemen, when she flashed it on them after being told the way somewhere, became of a sudden gayer, happier policemen and sang as they directed the traffic. Beggars, receiving it as a supplement to a small donation, perked up like magic and started to bite the ears of the passers-by with an abandon that made all the difference. And when they saw that smile even babies in their perambulators stopped looking like peevish poached eggs and became almost human.

(From *Sam the Sudden*, chapter 12)

'She went out in the Park to look at rabbits,' said Syd.

'Never seen one before. Not running about, that is, with all its insides in it.'

(From *If I Were You*, chapter 3)

Lord Ickenham patted her head, put his arm about her waist and kissed her tenderly. Pongo wished he had thought of that. He reflected moodily that this was always the way. In the course of their previous adventures together, if there had ever been any kissing or hand-patting or waist-encircling to be done, it had always been his nimbler uncle who had nipped in ahead of him and attended to it.

(From *Uncle Fred in the Springtime*, chapter 6)

'There are moments, Jeeves, when one asks oneself "Do trousers matter?".'

'The mood will pass, sir.'

(From *The Code of the Woosters*, chapter 5)

[My Uncle Tom] has a peculiarity I've noticed in other very oofy men. Nick him for the paltriest sum, and he lets out a squawk you can hear at Land's End. He has the stuff in gobs, but he hates giving it up.

(From *Right Ho, Jeeves*, chapter 7)

When government assessors call
To try and sneak your little all
You simply hit them with an axe
It's how you pay your income tax
In Bongo, it's on the Congo
And I wish that I was there.

(From 'Bongo on the Congo', a lyric from *Sitting Pretty*)

Judges, as a class, display, in the matter of arranging alimony, that reckless generosity which is only found in men who are giving away someone else's cash.

(From 'Fashionable Weddings and Smart Divorces' in *Louder and Funnier*)

'I attribute my whole success in life to a rigid observance of the fundamental rule:– Never have yourself tattooed with any woman's name, not even her initials.'

(From *French Leave*, chapter 3)

Inherited wealth does not, of course, make a young man nobler or more admirable, but the young man does not always know this.

(From *A Gentleman of Leisure*, chapter 1)

Ann detached a piece of cake and dropped it before the Peke. The Peke sniffed at it disparagingly, and resumed its steady gaze. It wanted chicken. It is the simple creed of the Peke that, where two human beings are gathered together to eat, chicken must enter into the proceedings somewhere.

(From *Big Money*, chapter 11)

It is fortunate that the quality of country house turbot is such that you do not notice much difference when it turns to ashes in your mouth, for this is what Monty's turbot was doing now.

(From *Heavy Weather*, chapter 15)

The first rule in buying Christmas presents is to select something shiny. If the chosen object is of leather, the leather must look as if it had been well greased; if of silver, it must gleam with the light that never was on sea or land. This is because the wariest person will often mistake shininess for expensiveness.

(From 'Happy Christmas and Merry New Year' in *Louder and Funnier*)

One of the things that being engaged does to you . . . is to fill you to the gills with a sort of knightly chivalry. . . . You go about the place like a Boy Scout, pouncing on passers-by and doing acts of kindness to them.

(From 'Trouble Down in Tudsleigh' in *Young Men in Spats*)

'This is a pretty state of affairs. . . . My daughter helping the foe of her family to fly—'

'Flee, father,' corrected the girl, faintly.

'Flea or fly – this is no time for arguing about insects.'

(From 'Romance of a Bulb-Squeezer' in *Meet Mr Mulliner*)

'. . . I find that I could put the whole dashed human race into a pit half a mile wide by half a mile deep.'

'I wouldn't,' said Jeff.

'No, don't,' said Anne. 'Think how squashy it would be for the ones at the bottom.'

(From *Money in the Bank*, chapter 6)

It just shows, what any member of Parliament will tell you, that if you want real oratory, the preliminary noggin is essential. Unless pie-eyed, you cannot hope to grip.

(From *Right Ho, Jeeves*, chapter 17)

[Galahad] had discovered the prime grand secret of eternal youth – to keep the decanter circulating and never go to bed before four in the morning.

(From *Full Moon*, chapter 3)

A head waiter makes good money, but he can always do with a devoted son who pays surtax.

(From *French Leave*, chapter 12)

'. . . And this,' he went on, bestowing a kindly glance on the glacial Valerie, 'is my favourite niece.'

'I'm your only niece.'

'Perhaps that's the reason,' said Lord Ickenham.

(From *Uncle Fred in the Springtime*, chapter 20)

As he kissed [his mother], [Ronnie Fish] was aware of something of the feeling which he had had in his boxing days when shaking hands with an unpleasant-looking opponent.

(From *Heavy Weather*, chapter 6)

Slingsby loomed in the doorway, like a dignified cloudbank.

(From *If I Were You*, chapter 1)

I attribute the insane arrogance of the later Roman emperors almost entirely to the fact that, never having played golf, they never knew that chastening humility which is engendered by a topped chip-shot. If Cleopatra had been outed in the first round of the Ladies' Singles, we should have heard a lot less of her proud imperiousness.

(From 'The Magic Plus-Fours' in *The Heart of a Goof*)

A man . . . who could stay indoors cataloguing vases while his fiancée wandered in the moonlight with explorers deserved all that was coming to him.

(From 'A Mixed Threesome' in *The Clicking of Cuthbert*)

Introduced to the child in the nursing-home, [Bingo] recoiled with a startled 'Oi!' and as the days went by the feeling that he had run up against something red-hot in no way diminished. The only thing that prevented a father's love from faltering was the fact that there was in his possession a photograph of himself at the same early age, in which he, too, looked like a homicidal fried egg.

(From 'Sonny Boy' in *Eggs, Beans and Crumpets*)

A melancholy-looking man, [he] had the appearance of one who has searched for the leak in life's gas-pipe with a lighted candle.

(From 'The Man who Disliked Cats' in *The Man Upstairs*)

'Love is a wonderful thing, Hash.'

Mr Todhunter's ample mouth curled sardonically.

'When you've seen as much of life as I have,' he replied, 'you'd rather have a cup of tea.'

(From *Sam the Sudden*, chapter 1)

'Love is like life assurance. The older you are when you start it, the more it costs.'

(From the play *Don't Listen, Ladies*)

'Some men decorate their home with old masters and others with old mistresses.'

(From the play *Don't Listen, Ladies*)

Into the face of the young man who sat on the terrace of the Hotel Magnifique at Cannes there had crept a look of furtive shame, the shifty, hangdog look which announces that an Englishman is about to talk French.

(From *The Luck of the Bodkins*, chapter 1)

He was gazing at the waitress with the look of a dog that's just remembered where its bone was buried.

(From 'Bingo and the Little Woman' in *The Inimitable Jeeves*)

'And go and get your hair cut,' screamed Beatrice. 'You look like a chrysanthemum.'

(From *Hot Water*, chapter 2)

Mike rather liked this way of putting it. It lent a certain dignity to the proceedings, making him feel like some important person for whose services there had been strenuous competition. He seemed to see the bank's directors being reassured by the chairman. ('I am happy to say, gentlemen, that our profits for the past year are £3,000,006-2-2½ – (cheers) – and' – impressively – 'that we have finally succeeded in inducing Mr Mike Jackson (sensation) – to – er – in fact, to join the staff!' (Frantic cheers, in which the chairman joined.))

(From *Psmith in the City*, chapter 4)

This girl talks French with both hands.

(From *Ring for Jeeves*, chapter 10)

As a child of eight Mr Trout had once kissed a girl of six under the mistletoe at a Christmas party, but there his sex life had come to an abrupt halt.

(From *Bachelors Anonymous*, chapter 9)

'We just happened to be sitting in a cemetery, and I asked her how she'd like to see my name on her tombstone.'

(From *If I Were You*, chapter 12)

'You're too clever for one man. You ought to incorporate.'

(From *The Small Bachelor*, chapter 10)

[Jill] had that direct, honest gaze which many nice girls have, and as a rule Bill liked it. But at the moment he could have done with something that did not pierce quite so like a red-hot gimlet to his inmost soul. A sense of guilt makes a man allergic to direct, honest gazes.

(From *Ring for Jeeves*, chapter 5)

There are girls, few perhaps but to be found if one searches carefully, who when their advice is ignored and disaster ensues, do not say 'I told you so'. Mavis was not of their number.

(From *Pearls, Girls and Monty Bodkin*, chapter 11)

In appearance Kelly was on the buxom side. In her middle forties she still retained much of the spectacular beauty of her youth, but a carelessness these last years in the matter of counting the calories had robbed her figure of its old streamlined look. Today she resembled a *Ziegfeld Follies* girl who had been left out in the rain and had swollen a little.

(From *Company for Henry*, chapter 3)

Honoria Glossop is one of those robust, dynamic girls with the muscles of a welter-weight and a laugh like a squadron of cavalry charging over a tin bridge.

(From 'The Rummy Affair of Old Biffy' in *Carry On, Jeeves*)

[36]

'Poverty is the banana-skin on the doorstep to romance.'

(From the lyric 'There isn't One Girl' in *Sitting Pretty*)

One of the rummy things about Jeeves is that, unless you watch like a hawk, you very seldom see him come into a room. He's like one of those weird birds in India who dissolve themselves into thin air and nip through space in a sort of disembodied way and assemble the parts again just where they want them. I've got a cousin who's what they call a Theosophist, and he says he's often nearly worked the thing himself, but couldn't quite bring it off, probably owing to having fed in his boyhood on the flesh of animals slain in anger and pie.

(From 'The Artistic Career of Corky' in *Carry On, Jeeves*)

'You're too young to marry,' [said Mr McKinnon, a stout bachelor.]

'So was Methuselah,' said James, a stouter.

(From 'Honeysuckle Cottage' in *Meet Mr Mulliner*)

Like so many substantial citizens of [America], he had married young and kept on marrying, springing from blonde to blonde like the chamois of the Alps leaping from crag to crag.

(From *Summer Moonshine*, chapter 2)

Between the courses he danced like something dark and slithery from the Argentine.

(From 'Feet of Clay' in *Nothing Serious*)

[Sergeant-Major Flannery's] moustache was long and blond and bushy, and it shot heavenwards into two glorious needle-point ends, a shining zareba of hair quite beyond the scope of any mere civilian. Non-army men may grow moustaches and wax them and brood over them and be fond and proud of them, but to obtain a waxed moustache in the deepest and holiest sense of the words you have to be a Sergeant-Major.

(From *Money for Nothing*, chapter 7)

'Many a man may look respectable, and yet be able to hide at will behind a spiral staircase.'

(From 'Success Story' in *Nothing Serious*)

Wilfred Allsop was sitting up, his face pale, his eyes glassy, his hair disordered. He looked like the poet Shelley after a big night out with Lord Byron.

(From *Galahad at Blandings*, chapter 1)

I admit any red-blooded Sultan or Pasha, if offered the opportunity of adding [Madeline Basset] to the personnel of his harem, would jump to it without hesitation, but he would regret his impulsiveness before the end of the first week. She's one of those soppy girls, riddled from head to foot with whimsy. She holds the view that the stars are God's daisy chain, that rabbits are gnomes in attendance on the Fairy Queen, and that every time a fairy blows its wee nose a baby is born, which, as we know, is not the case.

(From *Stiff Upper Lip, Jeeves*, chapter 2)

'He was stoutly opposed to the idea of marrying anyone; but if, as happens to the best of us, he ever were compelled to perform the wedding glide, he had always hoped it would be with some lady golf champion who would help him with his putting, and thus, by bringing his handicap down a notch or two, enable him to save something from the wreck.'

(From 'Honeysuckle Cottage' in *Meet Mr Mulliner*)

'Jeeves, I wish I had a daughter. I wonder what the procedure is.'

'Marriage is, I believe, considered the preliminary step, sir.'

(From 'Bertie Changes His Mind' in *Carry On, Jeeves*)

[41]

She found [him] seated at the table, playing chess with himself. From the contented expression on his face, he appeared to be winning.

(From *Money in the Bank*, chapter 3)

'All I said was "I know you started to learn to play bridge this morning, Reggie, but what time this morning?", but he didn't like it.'

(From *Do Butlers Burgle Banks?*, chapter 5)

There was the umpire with his hands raised, as if he were the Pope bestowing a blessing.

(From 'Tom, Dick and Harry' in *Grand Magazine*)

Freddie experienced the sort of abysmal soul-sadness which afflicts one of Tolstoi's Russian peasants when, after putting in a heavy day's work strangling his father, beating his wife, and dropping the baby into the city reservoir, he turns to the cupboard, only to find the vodka bottle empty.

(From *Jill the Reckless*, chapter 8)

It has been well said that an author who expects results from a first novel is in a position similar to that of a man who drops a rose petal down the Grand Canyon of Arizona and listens for the echo.

(From *Cocktail Time*, chapter 3)

[The silence was broken by] a crackling sound like a forest fire, as Mr Steptoe champed his toast. This gorilla-jawed man could get a certain amount of noise-response even out of mashed potatoes, but it was when eating toast that you caught him at his best.

(From *Quick Service*, chapter 1)

A false beard and spectacles [shielded] his identity from the public eye. If you asked him, he would have said he was a Scotch business man. As a matter of fact, he looked far more like a motor-car coming through a haystack.

(From 'Bill the Bloodhound' in *The Man with Two Left Feet*)

It is pretty generally admitted that Geoffrey Chaucer, the eminent poet of the fourteenth century, though obsessed with an almost Rooseveltian passion for the new spelling, was there with the goods when it came to profundity of thought.

(From 'Rough-Hew Them How We Will' in *The Man Upstairs*)

I am not a married man myself, so have no experience of how it feels to have one's wife whizz off silently into the unknown; but I should imagine that it must be something like taking a full swing with a brassie and missing the ball.

(From 'Sundered Hearts' in *The Clicking of Cuthbert*)

'George Cyril Wellbeloved is as mad as a March hatter. . . . It was his grandfather, Ezekiel Wellbeloved, who took off his trousers one snowy afternoon in the High Street and gave them to a passer-by, saying he wouldn't be needing them any longer, as the end of the world was coming that evening at five-thirty sharp.'

(From *Pigs Have Wings*, chapter 10)

. . . a tough-looking man in one of those tight suits which somehow seem to suggest dubious morals.

(From *Hot Water*, chapter 1)

'I may as well tell you . . . that if you are going about the place thinking things pretty, you will never make a modern poet. Be poignant, man, be poignant!'

(From *The Small Bachelor*, chapter 1)

Musical comedy is the Irish stew of drama. Anything may be put in it, with the certainty that it will improve the general effect.

(From 'Bill the Bloodhound' in *The Man with Two Left Feet*)

'You can't go by what a girl says, when she's giving you the devil for making a chump of yourself. It's like Shakespeare. Sounds well but doesn't mean anything.'

(From *Joy in the Morning*, chapter 16)

'What's that thing of Shakespeare's about someone having an eye like Mother's?'

'An eye like Mars, to threaten and command, is possibly the quotation for which you are groping, sir.'

(From *The Mating Season*, chapter 8)

[Aunt Dahlia] guffawed more liberally than I had ever heard a woman guffaw. If there had been an aisle, she would have rolled in it.

(From *Much Obliged, Jeeves*, chapter 9)

The Duke's moustache was rising and falling like seaweed on an ebb tide.

(From *Uncle Fred in the Springtime*, chapter 13)

[48]

Poets, as a class, are business men. Shakespeare describes the poet's eye as rolling in fine frenzy from heaven to earth, from earth to heaven, and giving to airy nothing a local habitation and a name, but in practice you will find that one corner of that eye is generally glued to the royalty returns.

(From *Uncle Fred in the Springtime*, chapter 13)

The ordinary man who is paying instalments on the *Encyclopaedia Britannica* is apt to get over-excited and to skip impatiently to Volume XXVIII (Vet-Zym) to see how it all comes out in the end.

(From 'The Man with Two Left Feet'
in *The Man with Two Left Feet*)

From the vicar's own lips he had had it officially that the [Mothers' Outing] expedition should drive to the neighbouring village of Bottsford Mortimer, where there were the ruins of an old abbey, replete with interest; lunch among these ruins; visit the local museum; . . . and, after filling in with a bit of knitting, return home. And now the whole trend of the party appeared to be towards the Amusement Park on the Bridmouth pier.

(From 'Tried in the Furnace' in *Young Men in Spats*)

[The swan made] a hissing noise like a tyre bursting in a nest of cobras.

(From 'Jeeves and the Impending Doom' in *Very Good, Jeeves*)

'Hang it!' said Bill to himself in the cab. 'I'll go to America!' The exact words probably which Columbus had used, talking the thing over with his wife.

(From *Uneasy Money*, chapter 1)

The village of Brookport, Long Island, is a summer place. It lives, like the mosquitoes that infest it, entirely on its summer visitors.

(From *Uneasy Money*, chapter 5)

On paper, Blair Eggleston was bold, cold and ruthless. Like so many of our younger novelists, his whole tone was that of a disillusioned, sardonic philanderer who had drunk the wine-cup of illicit love to its dregs but was always ready to fill up again and have another. There were passages in some of his books, notably *Worm i' the Root* and *Offal*, which simply made you shiver, so stark was their cynicism, so brutal the force with which they tore away the veils and revealed Woman as she is.

Deprived of his fountain-pen, however, Blair was rather timid with women. He had never actually found himself alone in an incense-scented studio with a scantily-clad princess reclining on a tiger skin, but in such a situation he would most certainly have taken a chair as near to the door as possible and talked about the weather.

(From *Hot Water*, chapter 14)

Now, seeing her weeping and broken before him, with all the infernal cheek which he so deprecated swept away on a wave of woe, his heart softened. It has been a matter of speculation among historians what Wellington would have done if Napoleon had cried at Waterloo.

(From *Sam the Sudden*, chapter 23)

. . . Mrs Pett, like most other people, subconsciously held the view that the ruder a person is the more efficient he must be. It is but rarely that anyone is found who is not dazzled by the glamour of incivility.

(From *Piccadilly Jim*, chapter 17)

'Can you lend me a comb?'

'What do you want with a comb?'

'I got some soup in my hair at lunch.'

(From 'The Story of Webster' in *Mulliner Nights*)

The aunt made a hobby of collecting dry seaweed, which she pressed and pasted in an album. One sometimes thinks that aunts live entirely for pleasure.

(From 'The Rough Stuff' in *The Clicking of Cuthbert*)

Aunt Dahlia . . . was gazing at [Jeeves] like a bear about to receive a bun.

(From *Jeeves and the Feudal Spirit*, chapter 12)

They train bank clerks to stifle emotion, so they will be able to refuse overdrafts when they become managers.

(From 'Ukridge's Accident Syndicate' in *Ukridge*)

'[Lord Emsworth] dislikes competent secretaries. They bother him and get on his nerves. They keep him from evading his responsibilities.'

(From *Galahad at Blandings*, chapter 2)

The private investigator who learns that he is saving a client a hundred thousand dollars is a private investigator who puts his prices up.

(From *Something Fishy*, chapter 19)

. . . so remarkable was this girl's loveliness that Mr Gedge momentarily forgot his troubles and unconsciously straightened his tie. House-broken husband though he was, he still had an eye for beauty.

(From *Hot Water*, chapter 12)

Marriage is a battlefield, not a bed of roses. . . . The only way of ensuring a happy married life is to get it thoroughly clear at the outset who is going to skipper the team. My own dear wife settled the point during the honeymoon, and ours has been an ideal union.

(From *Uncle Fred in the Springtime*, chapter 17)

One of the young men who had had to pick up the heart he had flung at Ann's feet and carry it away for repairs had once confided to an intimate friend, after the sting had to some extent passed, that the feelings of a man who made love to Ann might be likened to the emotions which hot chocolate might be supposed to entertain on contact with vanilla ice cream.

(From *Piccadilly Jim*, chapter 7)

It is an unnerving thing to be despised by a red-haired girl whose life you have just saved.

(From *Piccadilly Jim*, chapter 6)

. . . I seemed to note in his aspect a certain gravity, as if he had just discovered schism in his flock or found a couple of choirboys smoking reefers in the churchyard.

(From *Stiff Upper Lip, Jeeves*, chapter 3)

He tottered blindly towards the bar like a camel making for an oasis after a hard day at the office.

(From 'Life with Freddie' in *Plum Pie*)

He gave me the sort of look a batsman gives an umpire when he gives him out leg-before-wicket.

(From 'Concealed Art' in *Strand Magazine*)

He perceived that he was up against French red tape, compared to which that of Great Britain and America is only pinkish. Where in the matter of rules and regulations London and New York merely scratch the surface, these Gauls plumb the depths. It is estimated that a French minor official, with his heart really in his work, can turn more hairs grey and have more clients tearing those hairs than any six of his opposite numbers on the pay rolls of other nations.

(From *Frozen Assets*, chapter 1)

In a really civilised community crooners would be shot on sight.

(From *Quick Service*, chapter 5)

'It isn't so much his dancing on my feet that I mind – it's the way he jumps on and off that slays me.'

(From *Money for Nothing*, chapter 4)

[Esmond Haddock] looked like a combination of a poet and an all-in wrestler. It would not have surprised you to learn that [he] was the author of sonnet sequences of a fruity and emotional nature which had made him the toast of Bloomsbury, for his air was that of a man who could rhyme 'love' and 'dove' as well as the next chap. Nor would you have been astonished if informed that he had recently felled an ox with a single blow. You would simply have felt what an ass the ox must have been to get into an argument with a fellow with a chest like that.

(From *The Mating Season*, chapter 6)

It is the boast of Barribault's Hotel . . . that it can make the wrong sort of client feel more like a piece of cheese – and a cheap yellow piece of cheese at that – than any other similar establishment in the world. The personnel of its staff are selected primarily for their ability to curl the upper lip and raise the eyebrows just that extra quarter of an inch which makes all the difference.

(From *Full Moon*, chapter 3)

I doubt if golfers ought to fall in love.

(From 'Scratch Man' in *A Few Quick Ones*)

'You don't know anything about anything,' Mr Pynsent pointed out gently. 'It is the effect of your English public school education.'

(From *Sam the Sudden*, chapter 1)

'I've seen the light,' [said the policeman, hitherto an atheist,] 'and what I wanted to ask you, sir, was do I have to join the Infants' Bible Class or can I start singing in the choir right away?'

(From *The Mating Season*, chapter 26)

The butler was looking nervous, like Macbeth interviewing Lady Macbeth after one of her visits to the spare room.

(From 'Buried Treasure' in *Lord Emsworth and Others*)

He resembled a minor prophet who has been hit behind the ear by a stuffed eelskin.

(From 'Ukridge's Dog College' in *Ukridge*)

It's curious how, looking back, you can nearly always spot where you went wrong in any binge or enterprise. Take this little slab of community singing of ours, for instance. In order to give the thing zip, I stood on my chair and waved the decanter like a baton, and this, I see now, was a mistake. It helped the composition enormously, but it tended to create a false impression in the mind of the observer, conjuring up a picture of drunken revels.

(From *The Mating Season*, chapter 6)

'You'll be as cosy in here as a worm in a chestnut.'

(From *The Luck of the Bodkins*, chapter 10)

[Jerry Mitchell] knew that, in his wooing of Mrs Pett's maid, Celestine, he was handicapped by his looks, concerning which he had no illusions. No Adonis to begin with, he had been so edited and re-edited during a long and prosperous ring career by the gloved fists of a hundred foes that in affairs of the heart he was obliged to rely exclusively on moral worth and charm of manner.

(From *Piccadilly Jim*, chapter 1)

He looked like a Volga boatman who has just learned that Stalin has purged his employer.

(From 'Excelsior' in *Nothing Serious*)

'Chumps always make the best husbands. When you marry, Sally, grab a chump. . . . All the unhappy marriages come from the husband having brains. What good are brains to a man? They only unsettle him.'

(From *The Adventures of Sally*, chapter 10)

'Are wives often like that[, Jeeves]? Welcoming criticism of the lord and master, I mean?'

'They are generally open to suggestions from the outside public with regard to the improvement of their husbands, sir.'

'That is why married men are wan, what?'

'Yes, sir.'

(From 'Jeeves and the Old School Chum' in *Very Good, Jeeves*)

'You told them you were expecting to sell a hundred thousand copies?'

'We always tell them we're expecting to sell a hundred thousand copies,' said Russell Clutterbuck, letting him in on one of the secrets of the publishing trade.

(From *French Leave*, chapter 8)

They had all gone on to the opening performance at the Flaming Youth Group Centre of one of those avant-garde plays which bring the scent of boiling cabbage across the footlights and in which the little man in the bowler hat turns out to be God.

(From *Service with a Smile*, chapter 8)

'I am not going to marry Lord Rowcester,' she said curtly.

It seemed to Colonel Wyvern that his child must be suffering from some form of amnesia, and he set himself to jog her memory.

'Yes, you are,' he reminded her. 'It was in *The Times*.'

(From *Ring for Jeeves*, chapter 16)

[Beach's bullfinch] continued to chirp reflectively to itself, like a man trying to remember a tune in his bath.

(From *Summer Lightning*, chapter 3)

'I was one of those men my mother always warned me against.'

(From *Sunset at Blandings*, chapter 8)

'Don't talk rot, old Tom Travers.'

'I'm not accustomed to talk rot,' he said.

'Then, for a beginner,' I said, 'you do it dashed well.'

(From *Right Ho, Jeeves*, chapter 17)

'He wouldn't marry an heiress.'

'What!' cried Reggie, who would have married a dozen had the law permitted it.

(From *The Luck of the Bodkins*, chapter 15)

'Why do you want a political career? Have you ever been in the House of Commons and taken a good look at the inmates? As weird a gaggle of freaks and sub-humans as was ever collected in one spot.'

(From *Cocktail Time*, chapter 4)

'. . . how is it that I can't remember whether I murdered somebody or not last night. It isn't the sort of thing your sober man would lightly forget. Have you ever murdered anybody, Bayliss?'

'No, sir.'

'Well, if you had, you would remember it next morning?'

'I imagine so, Mr James.'

(From *Piccadilly Jim*, chapter 4)

Some policemen are born grafters, some achieve graft and some have graft thrust upon them.

(From *A Gentleman of Leisure*, chapter 3)

[69]

'Do you mean to . . . tell me,' [cried Ukridge, profoundly stirred – as ever – by a tale of easy money], 'that some dashed paper paid you five quid simply because you sprained your ankle? Pull yourself together, old horse. Things like that don't happen.'

'It's quite true.'

'Can you show me the fiver?'

'No, because if I did you would try to borrow it.'

(From 'Ukridge's Accident Syndicate' in *Ukridge*)

It was one of those still evenings you get in the summer, when you can hear a snail clear its throat a mile away.

(From 'Jeeves Takes Charge' in *Carry On, Jeeves*)

A woman is only a woman, but a frothing pint is a drink.

(From *Pigs Have Wings*, chapter 6)

Conversation on the [New York] Subway is impossible. The ingenious gentlemen who constructed it started with the object of making it noisy. Not ordinarily noisy, like a ton of coal falling onto a sheet of tin, but really noisy. So they fashioned the pillars of thin steel, and the sleepers of thin wood, and loosened all the nuts, and now a Subway train in motion suggests a prolonged dynamite explosion blended with the voice of some great cataract.

(From *Psmith, Journalist*, chapter 14)

'[Angelica Vining] wanted to borrow my aunt's brooch,' [said Ukridge,] 'but I was firm and wouldn't let her have it – partly on principle and partly because I had pawned it the day before.'

(From 'Ukridge and the Home from Home' in *Lord Emsworth and Others*)

Veronica Wedge was one of those girls who, if they have not plenty of precious stones on their person, feel nude.

(From *Galahad at Blandings*, chapter 7)

[He eyed] a sunbeam as if it wanted to borrow money from him.

(From *Big Money*, chapter 4)

The trouble with talking to a sister like a Dutch uncle is that she is very apt to come right back at you and start talking to you like a Dutch aunt.

(From *Pigs Have Wings*, chapter 2)

There would have been serious trouble between David and Jonathan if either had persisted in dropping catches off the other's bowling.

(From *Mike*, chapter 17)

[In boxing,] the right cross-counter is distinctly one of those things which it is more blessed to give than to receive.

(From *The Pothunters*, chapter 1)

'Yes,' said Millicent, rather in the tone of voice which Schopenhauer would have used when announcing the discovery of a caterpillar in his salad.

(From *Summer Lightning*, chapter 11)

'If you're thinking of the pudding, I'm afraid that's off. The kitten fell into the custard.'

'No!'

'She did. And when I'd fished her out there wasn't hardly any left. Seemed to have soaked into her like as if she was a sponge. Still, there 'ud be enough for you if Mr Wrenn didn't want any.'

(From *Sam the Sudden*, chapter 2)

Like all antique shops . . . [it was] dingy outside and dark and smelly within. I don't know why it is, but the proprietors of these establishments always seem to be cooking some sort of stew in the back room.

(From *The Code of the Woosters*, chapter 1)

Why is there unrest in India? Because its inhabitants eat only an occasional handful of rice. The day when Mahatma Gandhi sits down to a good juicy steak and follows it up with roly-poly pudding and a spot of Stilton you will see the end of all this nonsense of Civil Disobedience.

(From 'The Juice of an Orange' in *Blandings Castle and Elsewhere*)

'. . . If you were a millionaire, would you rather be stabbed in the back with a paperknife or found dead without a mark on you, staring with blank eyes at some appalling sight?'

(From 'Strychnine in the Soup' in *Mulliner Nights*)

It's the old problem, of course – the one that makes life so tough for murderers – what to do with the body.

(From *The Code of the Woosters*, chapter 12)

'South Kensington . . . where sin stalks naked through the dark alleys and only might is right.'

(From *Service with a Smile*, chapter 2)

'A woman's smile is like a bath-tap. Turn it on and you find yourself in hot water.'

(From the play *Candlelight*)

There is probably nothing so stimulating to a young fiancé . . . as the knowledge that he has got his story ready and that it will be impossible for the most captious critic to punch holes in it.

(From *Ice in the Bedroom*, chapter 11)

'I had a private income - the young artist's best friend.'

(From *Quick Service*, chapter 9)

England was littered with the shrivelled remains of curates at whom the lady bishopess had looked through her lorgnette. He had seen them wilt like salted snails at the episcopal breakfast-table.

(From 'Mulliner's Buck-U-Uppo' in *Meet Mr Mulliner*)

Of the myriad individuals that went to make up the kaleidoscopic life of New York, [Mrs Waddington] disliked artists most. They never had any money. They were dissolute and feckless. They attended dances at Webster Hall in strange costumes, and frequently played the ukelele.

(From *The Small Bachelor*, chapter 3)

Mrs Crocker bowed stiffly. She was thinking how hopelessly American Mr Pitt was; how baggy his clothes looked; what absurdly shaped shoes he wore; how appalling his hat was; how little hair he had; and how deplorably he lacked all those graces of repose, culture, physical beauty, refinement, dignity and mental alertness which raise men above the level of the common cockroach.

(From *Piccadilly Jim*, chapter 3)

'I don't know if you are a student of history, Corky, but if you are,' [said Ukridge], 'you'll agree with me that half the trouble in this world has come from women speaking ill-judged words.'

(From 'Ukridge and the Home from Home'
in *Lord Emsworth and Others*)

She could never forget that the man she loved was a man with a past. [He had been a poet.] Deep down in her soul there was always the corroding fear lest at any moment a particularly fine sunset or the sight of a rose in bud might undo all the work she had done, sending Rodney hotfoot once more to his *Thesaurus* and rhyming dictionary. It was for this reason that she always hurried him indoors when the sun began to go down and refused to have rose trees in her garden.

(From 'Rodney has a Relapse' in *Nothing Serious*)

[He had] never acted in his life and couldn't play the pin in *Pinafore*.

(From *The Luck of the Bodkins*, chapter 14)

This made him two up and three to play. What the average golfer would consider a commanding lead. But Archibald was no average golfer. A commanding lead for him would have been two up and one to play.

(From 'Archibald's Benefit' in *The Man Upstairs*)

'Cats are not dogs!'

(From 'The Story of Webster' in *Mulliner Nights*)

The fascination of shooting as a sport depends almost wholly on whether you are at the right or wrong end of a gun.

(From 'Unpleasantness at Bludleigh Court' in *Mr Mulliner Speaking*)

'. . . I must ask you in future to try to synchronise your arrival at the office with that of the rest of the staff. We aim as far as possible at the communal dead heat.'

(From *Ice in the Bedroom*, chapter 2)

'It was over a hundred in the shade.'

'You shouldn't have stayed in the shade,' said Freddie.

(From *If I Were You*, chapter 1)

'Travel is highly educational, sir.'

'I can't do with any more education. I was full up years ago.'

(From *The Code of the Woosters*, chapter 1)

As Egbert from boyhood up had shown no signs of possessing any intelligence whatsoever, a place had been found for him in the Civil Service.

(From 'A Christmas Carol', in *The World of Mr Mulliner*)

On [Constable Potter's] face was that hard, keen look which comes into the faces of policemen when they intend to do their duty pitilessly and crush a criminal like a snake beneath the heel. It was the look which Constable Potter's face wore when he was waiting beneath a tree to apprehend a small boy who was up in its branches stealing apples, the merciless expression that turned it to flint when he called at a house to serve a summons on somebody for moving pigs without a permit.

(From *Uncle Dynamite*, chapter 7)

Bottleton East is crammed from end to end with costermongers dealing in tomatoes, potatoes, Brussels sprouts and fruits in their season, and it is a very negligent audience there that forgets to attend a place of entertainment with full pockets.

(From 'The Masked Troubadour' in *Lord Emsworth and Others*)

Lady Hermione Wedge was . . . short and dumpy and looked like a cook – in her softer moods a cook well satisfied with her latest soufflé; when stirred to anger a cook about to give notice; but always a cook of strong character.

(From *Galahad at Blandings*, chapter 2)

Monte Carlo is a place to which everybody goes once in his life. It is the one spot in the world where a man may get something for nothing. You are bound to catch its fascination like measles and, also like measles, you are not likely to catch it more than once.

(From 'The Small Gambler' in *Louder and Funnier*)

Coming down to first causes, the only reason why collisions of any kind occur is because two bodies defy Nature's law that a given spot on a given plane shall at a given moment of time be occupied by only one body.

(From *Something Fresh*, chapter 8)

The RMS *Atlantic* [was behaving] more like a Russian dancer than a respectable ship. Ivor Llewellyn, prone in his bunk and holding on to the woodwork, was able to count no fewer than five occasions when the vessel lowered Nijinsky's record for leaping in the air and twiddling the feet before descending.

(From *The Luck of the Bodkins*, chapter 13)

Joe Bender was looking terrible. A man, to use an old-fashioned phrase, of some twenty-eight summers, he gave the impression at the moment of having experienced at least that number of very hard winters.

(From *A Pelican at Blandings*, chapter 6)

'Biff [Christopher]'s going to buy the *Thursday Review*, and put me in as editor, and that's a job I can hardly fail to hold down. I'm not likely to fire myself. If at first I make a mistake or two, I shall be very lenient and understanding.'

(From *Frozen Assets*, chapter 10)

'This,' he said, 'is like being in heaven without going to all the bother and expense of dying.'

(From *Hot Water*, chapter 18)

The usual drawback to success is that it annoys one's friends so.

(From 'The Man Upstairs' in *The Man Upstairs*)

[Aunt Dahlia] looked like a tomato struggling for self-expression.

(From *Right Ho, Jeeves*, chapter 20)

[Lady Malvern] fitted into my biggest armchair as if it had been built round her by someone who knew they were wearing armchairs tight about the hips that season.

(From 'Jeeves and the Unbidden Guest' in *Carry On, Jeeves*)

'Sisters are a mistake, Clarence. You should have set your face against them from the outset.'

(From *Pigs Have Wings*, chapter 1)

It is a curious fact, and one frequently noted by
philosophers, that every woman in this world cherishes
within herself a deep-rooted belief, from which nothing
can shake her, that the particular man to whom she has
plighted her love is to be held personally blameworthy for
practically all of the untoward happenings of life.

(From *Sam the Sudden*, chapter 29)

He had studied Woman, and he knew that when Woman
gets into a tight place her first act is to shovel the blame off
onto the nearest male.

(From 'Trouble Down in Tudsleigh' in *Young Men in Spats*)

'My dear Ronald! . . . That tie!'

Ronnie Fish gazed at her lingeringly. It needed, he felt, but this. Poison was running through his veins, his world was rocking, green-eyed devils were shrieking mockery in his ears, and along came blasted aunts babbling of ties. It was as if somebody had touched Othello on the arm as he poised the pillow and criticised the cut of his doublet.

(From *Heavy Weather*, chapter 6)

Hash [looked] like one who has drained the four-ale of life and found a dead mouse at the bottom of the pewter.

(From *Sam the Sudden*, chapter 21)

If there is one thing in this world that should be done quickly or not at all, it is the removal of one's personal snake from the bed of a comparative stranger.

(From 'Something Squishy' in *Mr Mulliner Speaking*)

It seems to be one of Nature's laws that the most attractive girls should have the least attractive brothers.

(From *The Adventures of Sally*, chapter 1)

What magic there is in a girl's smile. It is the raisin which, dropped in the yeast of male complacency, induces fermentation.

(From *The Girl on the Boat*, chapter 3)

He continued to fold her in his arms, but it was with a growing feeling that he wished she had been a steak smothered in onions.

(From *Summer Moonshine*, chapter 24)

A fruity voice, like old tawny port made audible, said 'Come in'.

(From *Something Fresh*, chapter 5)

'I say, Moke,' said Rory, 'can you speak Spanish?'

'I don't know, I've never tried.'

(From *Ring for Jeeves*, chapter 9)

In most English country towns, if the public houses do not actually outnumber the inhabitants, they all do an excellent trade. It is only when they are two to one that hard times hit them and set the inn-keepers blaming the Government.

(From *Something Fresh*, chapter 7)

Aberdeen terriers, possibly owing to their heavy eyebrows, always seem to look at you as if they were in the pulpit of the church of some particularly strict Scottish sect and you were a parishioner of dubious reputation sitting in the front row of the stalls.

(From *Stiff Upper Lip, Jeeves*, chapter 8)

'He is a mere uncouth Cossack.'

A Cossack, I knew, was one of those things clergymen wear, and I wondered why [Florence] thought Stilton was like one.

(From *Joy in the Morning*, chapter 18)

' . . . [Ronnie Fish] travelled back to Paris with [Myra Schoonmaker] and left her there.'

'How fickle men are!' sighed Millicent.

(From *Summer Lightning*, chapter 1)

What [Jill Willard] did not know of the methods of the criminal classes could have been written on a bloodstain.

(From *Do Butlers Burgle Banks*, chapter 3)

'You can't go by what a man in my position promises. You don't really suppose, do you, that you can run a big [movie] studio successfully if you go about keeping your promise all the time.'

(From *Pearls, Girls and Monty Bodkin*, chapter 12)

Two heads, unless of course severed, are so often better than one.

(From *Pigs Have Wings*, chapter 9)

[His niece Angela] was a pretty girl, with fair hair and blue eyes which in their softer moments probably reminded all sorts of people of twin lagoons slumbering beneath a southern sky. This, however, was not one of those moments. To Lord Emsworth, as they met his, they looked like something out of an oxy-acetylene blowpipe.

(From 'Pig-Hoo-o-o-o-ey' in *Blandings Castle and Elsewhere*)

He looked haggard and care-worn, like a Borgia who has suddenly remembered that he has forgotten to put cyanide in the consommé, and the dinner gong due any minute.

(From 'Clustering Round Young Bingo' in *Carry On, Jeeves*)

All rather stout automobile manufacturers are sad when there is a full moon.

(From *Uneasy Money*, chapter 10)

I am a man who can read faces, and Chuffy's had seemed to me highly suggestive. Not only had its expression, as he spoke of Pauline, been that of a stuffed frog with a touch of the Soul's Awakening about it, but it had also turned a fairly deepish crimson in colour. The tip of the nose had wiggled, and there had been embarrassment in the manner. The result being that I had become firmly convinced that the old schoolmate had copped it properly.

(From *Thank You, Jeeves*, chapter 4)

He heaved himself up in slow motion like a courtly hippopotamus rising from its bed of reeds on a riverbank.

(From *Something Fishy*, chapter 2)

I was stunned. I began to understand how a general must feel when he has ordered a regiment to charge and has been told that it isn't in the mood.

(From *Right Ho, Jeeves*, chapter 13)

He was staring increduously, like one bitten by a rabbit.

(From *The Code of the Woosters*, chapter 7)

Just as all American publishers hope that if they are good and lead upright lives, their books will be banned in Boston, so all English publishers pray that theirs will be denounced from the pulpit by a bishop. Full statistics are not to hand, but it is estimated by competent judges that a good bishop, denouncing from the pulpit with the right organ note in his voice, can add between ten and fifteen thousand to the sales.

(From *Cocktail Time*, chapter 3)

She looked like something that might have occurred to Ibsen in one of his less frivolous moments.

(From *Summer Lightning*, chapter 8)

[Ricky Gilpin turned on the Duke of Dunstable.] 'You are without exception the worst tick and bounder that ever got fatty degeneration of the heart through half a century of gorging food and swilling wine wrenched from the lips of a starving proletariat. You make me sick. You poison the air. Good-bye, Uncle Alaric,' said Ricky, drawing himself away rather ostentatiously. 'I think we had better terminate this interview, or I may become brusque.'

(From *Uncle Fred in the Springtime*, chapter 13)

Walter clasped her to his bosom, using the interlocking grip.

(From 'Joy Bells for Walter' in *A Few Quick Ones*)

To attract attention in the dining-room of the Senior Conservative Club between the hours of one and two-thirty, you have to be a mutton-chop, not an Earl.

(From *Something Fresh*, chapter 3)

'If England wants a happy, well-fed aristocracy, she mustn't have wars. She can't have it both ways.'

(From *Big Money*, chapter 1)

Whatever may be said in favour of the Victorians, it is pretty generally admitted that few of them were to be trusted within reach of a trowel and a pile of bricks.

(From *Summer Moonshine*, chapter 2)

She goggled at me with all the open dismay of an aunt who has inadvertently bitten into a bad nut.

(From *Much Obliged, Jeeves*, chapter 10)

He misses short putts because of the uproar of the butterflies in the adjoining meadows.

(From 'Ordeal by Golf' in *The Clicking of Cuthbert*)

He spoke with a certain what-is-it in his voice, and I could see that, if not actually disgruntled, he was far from being gruntled, so I tactfully changed the subject.

(From *The Code of the Woosters*, chapter 1)

['That melting look,' she said,] 'seems to pump me full of vitamins. It makes me feel as if the sun was shining and my hat was right and my shoes were right and my frock was right and my stockings were right, and somebody had just left me ten thousand a year.'

(From *Spring Fever*, chapter 15)

Ernest Plinlimmon was not one of your butterflies who flit from flower to flower. He was an average-adjuster, and average-adjusters are like chartered accountants. When they love, they give their hearts for ever.

(From 'There's Always Golf' in *Lord Emsworth and Others*)

'We have no evidence whatsoever that Sir Galahad was ever called upon to do anything half as dangerous [as stopping a dog-fight]. And anyway, he wore armour. Give me a suit of mail, reaching well down over the ankles, and I will willingly intervene in a hundred dog-fights. But in thin flannel trousers, no!'

(From *The Girl on the Boat*, chapter 3)

It was one of those hairy, nondescript dogs, and its gaze was cold, wary and suspicious, like that of a stockbroker who thinks someone is going to play the confidence trick on him.

(From 'Lord Emsworth and the Girl Friend'
in *Blandings Castle and Elsewhere*)

It is not easy to look careworn when you are balancing a walking stick on the top of your nose, but Bill Oakshott contrived to do so.

(From *Uncle Dynamite*, chapter 11)

'Spode's one of those silver-tongued orators you read about. Extraordinary gift of the gab he has. He could get into Parliament without straining a sinew.' . . .

'Then why doesn't he?'

'He's a lord.'

'Don't they allow lords in?'

'No, they don't.'

'I see,' I said, rather impressed by this proof that the House of Commons drew the line somewhere.

(From *Much Obliged, Jeeves*, chapter 6)

For an instant Wilfred Allsop's face lit up, as that of the poet Shelley whom he so closely resembled must have done when he suddenly realised that 'blithe spirit' rhymes with 'near it', not that it does, and another ode as good as off the assembly line.

(From *Galahad at Blandings*, chapter 6)

[A] young man with dark circles under his eyes was propping himself up against a penny-in-the-slot machine. An undertaker, passing at that moment, would have looked at this young man sharply, scenting business. So would a buzzard.

(From *The Luck of the Bodkins*, chapter 2)

'Things have come to a pretty pass,' [said Mr Schnellenhamer] with a dignity as impressive as it was simple, 'if a free-born American citizen cannot bribe the police of his native country.'

(From 'The Rise of Minna Nordstrom'
in *Blandings Castle and Elsewhere*)

' . . . father crawled out from under the sofa and gave me twopence, making threepence in all – a good morning's work. I bought father a diamond ring with it at a shop down the street, I remember. At least, I thought it was a diamond. They may have swindled me, for I was very young.'

(From *Leave It To Psmith*, chapter 3)

They moved off slowly with bowed heads, like a couple of pall-bearers who have forgotten their coffin and had to go back for it.

(From *The Mating Season*, chapter 22)

It has been well said of Sigsbee H Waddington that, if men were dominoes, he would be the double-blank.

(From *The Small Bachelor*, chapter 1)

[My predecessor] died of cirrhosis of the liver. It costs money to die of cirrhosis of the liver.

(From 'Success Story' in *Nothing Serious*)

Any line that is cut out of any actor's part is always the only good line he has.

(From *Jill the Reckless*, chapter 14)

. . . that sweetest triumph of an assistant master's life; the spectacle of one boy smacking another boy's head because the latter persists in making a noise after [the master] had told him to stop.

(From *The Little Nugget*, Part II chapter 2)

Too many cooks, in baking rock cakes, get misled by the word 'rock'.

(From *Money in the Bank*, chapter 5)

His air was that of a man who has been passed through a wringer, and his eyes, what you could see of them, had a strange, smouldering gleam. He was so encrusted with alluvial deposits that one realized how little a mere bath would ever be able to effect. To fit him to take his place in polite society, he would certainly have to be sent to the cleaner's. Indeed, it was a moot point whether it wouldn't be simpler just to throw him away.

(From 'The Ordeal of Young Tuppy' in *Very Good, Jeeves*)

He sat motionless, his soul seething within him like a welsh rarebit at the height of its fever.

(From 'Tangled Hearts' in *Nothing Serious*)

It is a good rule in life never to apologise. The right sort of people do not want apologies, and the wrong sort take a mean advantage of them.

(From 'The Man Upstairs' in *The Man Upstairs*)

'Listen, Nobby,' I said.

She didn't, of course. I've never met a girl yet who did. Say 'Listen' to any member of the delicately-nurtured sex, and she takes it as a cue to start talking herself.

(From *Joy in the Morning*, chapter 12)

I was so darned sorry for poor old Corky that I hadn't the heart to touch my breakfast. I told Jeeves to drink it himself.

(From 'Leave it to Jeeves' in *My Man Jeeves*)

Uncle Tom . . . always looked a bit like a pterodactyl with a secret sorrow.

(From *Right Ho, Jeeves*, chapter 9)

Sir Roderick sort of just waggled an eyebrow in my direction and I saw that it was back to the basket for Bertram. I never met a man who had such a knack of making a fellow feel like a waste-product.

(From 'The Rummy Affair of Old Biffy' in *Carry On, Jeeves*)

The brains of members of the Press departments of motion-picture studios resemble soup at a cheap restaurant. It is wiser not to stir them.

(From 'Monkey Business' in *Blandings Castle and Elsewhere*)

Few things in life are more embarrassing than the necessity of having to inform an old friend that you have just got engaged to his fiancée.

(From *Big Money*, chapter 9)

One leisured son-in-law struck him as sufficient. He was not bitten by a craze for becoming a collector.

(From 'A Job of Work' in *Strand Magazine*)

[The] girl before him was not pretty. She was distinctly plain. Even ugly. She looked as if she might be a stenographer selected for some business magnate by his wife out of a number of competing applicants.

(From 'Fate' in *Young Men in Spats*)

She was a conscientious secretary. . . . It was this defect in her character that so exasperated Lord Emsworth. His ideal secretary would have been one who breakfasted in bed, dozed in an armchair through the morning, played golf in the afternoon and took the rest of the day off.

(From *Galahad at Blandings*, chapter 11)

It was my Uncle George who discovered that alcohol was a food well in advance of modern medical thought.

(From 'The Delayed Exit of Claude and Eustace' in *The Inimitable Jeeves*)

One of the first lessons life teaches us is that on these occasions of back-chat between the delicately-nurtured a man should retire into the offing, curl up in a ball, and imitate the prudent tactics of the opossum, which, when danger is in the air, pretends to be dead, frequently going to the length of hanging out crêpe and instructing its friends to stand around and say what a pity it all is.

(From 'Jeeves and the Old School Chum' in *Very Good, Jeeves*)

He [gave] one of those short, quick, roopy coughs by means of which solicitors announce that a conference is concluded.

(From *Money in the Bank*, chapter 1)

[The Aberdeen terrier] gave me an unpleasant look and said something under its breath in Gaelic.

(From *The Code of the Woosters*, chapter 4)

'Do you know where little boys go who listen to private conversations?' said Jimmy, severely.

'To the witness stand generally, I guess.'

(From *Piccadilly Jim*, chapter 18)

Golf, like measles, should be caught young, for, if postponed to riper years, the results may be serious.

(From 'A Mixed Threesome' in *The Clicking of Cuthbert*)

. . . a corner of the Club reading room, which he had selected because silence was compulsory there, thus rendering it possible for two men to hear each other speak.

(From *Uneasy Money*, chapter 2)

There's only one real cure for grey hair. It was invented by a Frenchman. He called it the guillotine.

(From *The Old Reliable*, chapter 1)

Many a time in the past, when an active operator on [Wall] Street, he had done things to the small investor which would have caused raised eyebrows on the fo'c's'le of a pirate sloop - and done them without a blush.

(From 'Keeping in with Vosper' in *The Heart of a Goof*)

A youth and middle age spent on the London Stock Exchange had left Lester Carmody singularly broadminded. He had to a remarkable degree that spacious charity which allows a man to look indulgently on any financial project, however fishy, provided he can see a bit in it for himself.

(From *Money for Nothing*, chapter 5)

'What does this so-called "social life" amount to? Spending money you didn't earn for things you don't want, to impress people you don't like.'

(From the play *If I Were You*)

I've said it before and I'll say it again – girls are rummy. Old Pop Kipling never said a truer word than when he made that crack about the f of the s being more d than the m.

(From *Right Ho, Jeeves*, chapter 19)

'When it comes to love, there's a lot to be said for the *à la carte* as opposed to the *table d'hôte*.'

(From *Ring for Jeeves*, chapter 18)

[Mr Crocker had been enthusiastically explaining the game of baseball to Bayliss, an English butler.]

'Quite an interesting game,' said Bayliss. 'But I find, now that you have explained it, sir, that it is familiar to me, though I have always known it under another game. It is played a great deal in this country. . . . It is known in England as rounders, sir. Children play it with a soft ball and a racket, and derive considerable enjoyment from it. I have never heard of it before as a pastime for adults.'

(From *Piccadilly Jim*, chapter 2)

'This afternoon he asked me to be his wife, and I turned him down like a bedspread.'

(From 'The Right Approach' in *A Few Quick Ones*)